Mermaid

Underwater Magic

Sue Mongredien

Illustrated by Maria Pearson

For Holly Powell,
with lots of love from Mum.

First published in the UK in 2009 by Usborne Publishing Ltd., Usborne House,
83-85 Saffron Hill, London EC1N 8RT, England. www.usborne.com

A CIP catalogue record for this book is available from the British Library.

JF AMJJASON /09 88835

ISBN 9780746096178

Printed in Great Britain.

Contents

The **Mermaids** of the

Molly

Ella

Delphi

Shivana

Undersea Kingdom

Coral

Queen Luna

Princess Silva

Pearl

Chapter One

Molly Holmes jumped as rain suddenly lashed against the cottage window. She got up from the saggy old sofa in the living room to peer outside. It was early evening in midsummer, but already the sky was dark and bruised-looking, with dense grey and purple clouds. Raindrops pattered against the glass, sliding down it in long, glistening trails.

Her gran came to join her at the window.

"I don't think anyone will be taking a stroll
along Horseshoe Bay this evening," Gran joked,
slipping an arm around Molly.

"Nor paddling," Molly replied with a smile. The sea looked as dark and menacing as the sky, and huge white-crested waves were rolling in, crashing onto the sand. She shivered as she thought about how cold the damp sand would feel on bare skin.

"It's not the nicest evening, is it?" Molly's mum commented, coming to stand next to them with Toby, Molly's baby brother, in her arms. Toby had bright red spots on his cheeks and tears were spouting from his eyes. He kept putting his fingers in his mouth and crying. "All right, sweet pea," Molly's mum said, rocking him to and fro. "He's got his first tooth coming through," she explained to Molly. "I think we're probably in for a noisy night from this little man."

Molly's dad came in from the kitchen just then, carrying a tray laden with mugs of steaming hot chocolate and a plate of ginger biscuits.

He set the tray down, then glanced over at the fireplace, which hadn't been lit while Molly's family had been living in the cottage. "I'll go out to the shed and chop a few logs to make a fire soon," he said. "It doesn't feel like summer any more."

"Still, it could be worse," Molly's mum said, rocking Toby. "We could be out at sea. Imagine that, on a night like tonight! Thank goodness we'll be cosy and warm here instead."

Molly smiled to herself, not daring to reply. In truth, she hoped she *would* be at sea tonight – with her new mermaid friends!

Since Molly's family had moved in with her gran, Molly had discovered a wonderful secret. Sometimes, at night, she transformed into a mermaid – the new "secret mermaid", one of six special mermaid Shell-Keepers, just like her gran had been before her.

The Shell-Keeper
mermaids all had
fragments of the
same magical conch
shell; Gran had given
Molly her creamy-
white piece on a silver
chain the day Molly's
family had moved in. Molly hadn't
realized just how amazing a present it was until
that first night, when bright pink sparkles had
flooded out from the shell, and the mermaid
magic had begun, whisking Molly to the ocean
for an adventure she'd never forget!

Unfortunately, Molly had discovered from the
other Shell-Keepers that a bad mermaid known
as Carlotta the Dark Queen had stolen the other
five pieces of conch to use for her own wicked
ends. And, as the secret mermaid, Molly had to

help the other mermaids find them again. She'd already helped her friend Ella get her piece back, but there were still four fragments of conch missing – and Molly was desperate to return to the ocean and seek them out.

It was frustrating, Molly thought, that she couldn't just turn herself into a mermaid whenever she wanted to. She had to wait for the magic to come all on its own. But it did mean that she looked forward to going up to bed each night – she was always hopeful of another mermaid adventure!

She turned away from the storm outside the window. "I'll just go and get my pyjamas on," she told her parents, and Gran gave her a smile. Molly smiled back and went out of the room and up the narrow stairs. She would have loved to know more about Gran's adventures as a secret mermaid all those years ago, but she knew that Gran was forbidden to talk to anyone about them – just as she, Molly, had promised to keep quiet about the mermaids too. Somehow it made it all the more exciting, though, hugging such an amazing secret to herself.

When she'd said goodnight to her parents and Gran, she got into bed, and reached out to pick up her special shell. It felt cool and smooth in her palm, and she closed her eyes with a wistful smile. "I hope I can help you soon, mermaids," she murmured.

It took a long time for Molly to drift off that night. She tossed and turned in bed, but she kept hearing her brother's plaintive cries of pain from his bedroom next door. The storm was still raging outside too, with rain spattering against the window. Molly could hear the roar of the waves from her bed as they thundered against the rocks.

After a while, Molly opened her eyes. "I'm never going to get to sleep," she muttered to herself. But as she said the words, her conch began to glow with its magical pink light, and a mist of tiny golden sparkles appeared around the shell. "Oh!" gasped Molly in excitement and she shut her eyes at once. The mermaid magic was beginning again!

Chapter Two

Molly had been a mermaid twice before now, but she still wasn't used to the peculiar melting sensation as her body transformed. Her legs in particular felt as if they were dissolving into nothing – it was rather alarming! But then, suddenly, she could feel the coolness of seawater against her skin and she opened her eyes eagerly. Yes! She was a mermaid again. Her legs had vanished, and now she had her very own shimmering silver tail flicking behind her!

"Hello, Molly," came a voice from nearby. "I thought that was you!"

Molly turned to see Delphi, one of the other Shell-Keeper mermaids. Delphi had bobbed auburn hair, green eyes and a sprinkling of freckles over her nose. She wore a jade-green top, and had a pale green flower tucked in her hair.

"Hello!" Molly cried joyfully and swam over towards her. Something felt different though. Why was it so hard to swim all of a sudden? Usually, as a mermaid, Molly could speed through the water very fast.

Delphi noticed Molly struggle and came to meet her halfway. "The current is really strong today, isn't it?" she said. She hugged Molly in welcome. "There have been some terrible storms lately, too. Usually, my piece of the conch helps me protect sailors at sea – I can use its powers to guide their ships safely back to harbour. But without it, I haven't been able to do anything, and there have almost been some dreadful shipwrecks."

"Well, I can help you look for your shell," Molly said at once. "I— "

Before she could finish her sentence, though, a pod of dolphins had appeared, smiling as they dived down through the water towards the two mermaids.

"Ahh," Delphi murmured to Molly. "Here come my little helpers. Or rather, they *think* they're helping."

The first dolphin to reach them made some excited whistling, snickering noises to Delphi, its eyes bright and alert. Molly couldn't take her eyes off the beautiful creature. She could hardly believe she was so close to it!

"You think you've found the shell?" Delphi replied. "Okay, we'll follow you. Come on, Molly, let's see what they've got this time."

She flicked her tail fin and surged away through the water. Molly gave her own tail a sharp wiggle and swam after her. She was surprised that Delphi didn't seem more enthusiastic at the dolphin's message. "What's up?" she hissed to her as they followed the sleek, silvery dolphins.

Delphi gave a tired smile in reply. "I do love

the dolphins – they're so cheerful and bouncy and keen to help," she said in a low voice, "but they're a bit *too* keen to help, if you know what I mean. They've been in and out of the shipwrecks looking for my conch piece, and they keep thinking they've seen it, and coming to get me, when really it's just another piece of human treasure that they've discovered." She rolled her eyes comically. "What with them, and Princess Silva hanging around all the time asking if I've found the shell yet, I've hardly had a minute to myself."

Molly bit her lip, hoping she would be more help than the dolphins and Princess Silva. Maybe Delphi didn't even *want* her hanging around – maybe she was secretly wishing Molly hadn't turned up at all!

Delphi caught the doubtful expression on Molly's face and put a hand on her arm.

"Oh – I didn't mean I wanted to be on my own *now*!" she said quickly. "I heard how brilliant you were at helping Ella when she'd been thrown onto the sand by that scary killer whale. I'm really pleased you're here to help me, too – truly, Molly!"

Molly smiled in relief. "Oh good," she said. "I'm pleased to be here."

They swam on, and Molly remembered Delphi's earlier comment about Princess Silva, daughter of the Merqueen. Queen Luna was lovely, but there was something a bit odd about the princess, Molly thought privately. She always seemed to be hanging around in the background, listening and watching without saying very much. Maybe she was just a bit shy, though.

The dolphins had stopped before a huge rock on the seabed and were pointing their shiny noses at it, all making whistling noises at once.

"Okay, let's have a look," Delphi said in a good-humoured way. Molly could tell she didn't really believe her shell would be there.

But then Delphi's mouth fell open in surprise and her eyes lit up. "Oh! My conch! You really *did* find it!" she cried, and she threw her arms around the nearest dolphin, covering his head with happy kisses.

Molly swam over to the rock excitedly for a closer look. Sure enough, wedged into a crevice was Delphi's piece of the conch! The shell's creamy surface seemed to glow against the dark, barnacle-covered rock, and was half-hidden by a spiky round object that rested on top of it. Was the spiky thing some kind of plant? Molly wondered.

Delphi patted the other dolphins lovingly, then joined Molly in front of the rock. "At last!" she cried happily, reaching out a hand to move the spiky thing. "Oh, I've been so worried! And now—"

"Oi!" the spiky thing snapped in a bad-tempered way, making Molly jump back in alarm. "Get your hand away from me, or I'll jab you with my spines!"

Molly stared at the spiky thing and then questioningly at Delphi. "What *is* that?" she whispered.

"It's a sea urchin," Delphi replied in a low voice. "A grumpy sea urchin at that!"

She turned back to the creature. "But you're on my shell," she said to it politely. "Please would you move, so that I can get it?"

"No," the sea urchin told her. "It's mine now, I found it. Lovely and smooth it is, too, after that craggy old rock. Shouldn't have been so careless with it, should you?"

"Oh please," Molly put in. "It was stolen from her – she wasn't being careless!"

The sea urchin's red spines rippled in the current. They did look horribly sharp, Molly thought to herself. "I said no, and I mean no!" the sea urchin replied crossly. "And if either of you comes anywhere near me again, I'll jab you so hard, you'll be sorry!"

Chapter Three

Molly and Delphi looked at one another, then swam a little way away from the bad-tempered sea urchin. "A sea urchin's spines aren't poisonous, but they are painful and difficult to get out," Delphi said to Molly with a sigh. "And it means what it says too, I'm sure."

"Well, we'll just have to think of a way we can persuade it to move," Molly said, racking her brains for an idea. "And before the Dark

Queen finds out your conch is here, too."
Then the sea urchin's words came back to her.
"Lovely and smooth" it had called the shell.
So maybe if they could find something else
that was lovely and smooth, they might be
able to talk the sea urchin into swapping...

Molly whispered her idea to Delphi, who
clapped her hands. "Yes – that might just
work," she said. "Come on, let's see what the
old grouch thinks."

The two mermaids swam back to the

sea urchin, which
waggled its spines
threateningly
when it
sensed them
approaching.
"Now what?"
it asked sharply.

"I was just wondering," Molly said in her politest voice, "how you felt about swapping that old shell for something even better?"

"Something sparkly, perhaps," Delphi said coaxingly. "Your spines would look really good then, wouldn't they?"

The sea urchin hesitated. "What sort of sparkly thing?" it asked in a gruff voice.

"Treasure," Delphi told it. "I found some lovely pieces earlier. Smooth, shiny silver plates...some golden goblets you could make a cave out of... What do you think?"

There was an agonizing pause while the sea urchin considered this. Then it spoke. "Very well, then," it said. "But no trickery, mind!"

"No trickery," Molly promised solemnly. "Come on, Delphi, let's go on a treasure hunt."

The two mermaids swam away quickly, pleased that the sea urchin was being more reasonable.

29

Now they just had to find some treasure!

"I know the perfect place," Delphi told Molly. "There's a shipwreck not far from here. The dolphins were exploring it earlier; there are all sorts of treasures and trinkets there."

The mermaids swam on, and Molly's own piece of conch bobbed around on its chain. Her conch had already worked some powerful magic when she'd asked for its help in the past, and Molly was glad to have it with her.

The sea was still very hard to swim through. The current was stronger than ever, and Molly felt herself buffeted backwards by it, despite her muscular tail. "It's another storm," Delphi said anxiously, gazing up above them. "I can hear the rain from all the way down here."

"What's that?" Molly asked, seeing a huge dark object in the distance. "Is it some kind of ship?"

Delphi peered through the raging current. "It's an oil tanker," she said after a moment, and a look of horror crossed her face.

"What's it doing up there? It should be further out – there's a rocky outcrop not far from here."

Molly felt worried. She knew that an oil spill would mean disaster for the marine environment. "Do you think the tanker might hit the rocks?"

"Yes, if we can't get it back on course," Delphi replied, her mouth in a tense line. "Oh, we must get my conch quickly! Then I'll be able to quell the storm and guide the tanker back where it should be!"

"Come on," Molly said. "Let's grab some treasure for the sea urchin fast."

She and Delphi swam as hard as they could until they reached the shipwreck. The boat was wooden and very old, and lay at an angle, battered and broken on the seabed, with fish swimming in and out of the holes in its sides. There were still the remains of a mast and crossbeam standing, and even some of the old rigging floating from the beams.

Delphi dived through a gap in the ship's wrecked hull and Molly followed her, taking care to avoid the jagged edges.

Inside the main part of the ship, it was eerie and still. Molly couldn't help thinking about all the people who'd been on board when the ship had gone down. Now the wreck was home to starfish and sea anemones. Seaweed grew through the holes, the fronds swaying over the aged wood. But she wasn't here to sightsee, Molly reminded herself, as a vision of the oil tanker flashed into her mind. She and Delphi needed to find some treasure for the sea urchin – and quickly!

Molly saw a gleam of silver, half-buried beneath a large clump of bobbly seaweed and some fine pale sand, and dug away with her fingers to uncover a small silver dish. "I've found this!" she shouted to Delphi, holding it up. "What do you think?"

"Great, I'll put it in my bag," said Delphi, from further inside the ship. "Let's just open this chest and see what's inside too. We should take a few things with us in case that grouchy sea urchin doesn't like what we offer him. There might be something even better in here."

Molly saw that her friend was scrabbling to prise open an old metal chest which was tarnished and dented with age. Molly swam over and helped lift the rusted catch, using a mussel shell as a lever. "There!" she said, panting as the lid finally swung up with a creak.

"Ooh," Delphi said, peering inside. "Doubloons! Pirate gold!"

Molly reached in and took out a handful of the old coins, still gleaming gold after all their time underwater. "The chest must have been pretty watertight," she said. "They seem good as new!"

"Oh, and look what's underneath them," Delphi said, burrowing into the bright mound of coins. She held up a curved knife with a jewelled handle.

"A cutlass! This really must have been a pirate ship once upon a time." She ran a finger along the blade of the cutlass and shivered. "I think we'll leave that here, though," she said. She gathered up a handful of coins instead and slipped them, along with a ruby-studded golden goblet and the silver dish, into the little green bag she wore around one shoulder. "There. That'll do. Let's go!"

Molly closed the chest again, and followed Delphi up through a hole overhead. But as she swam back over the old deck of the shipwreck, she caught sight of a pair of red eyes glowing through the murky water ahead and her heart lurched with fear. Oh, no. The last time she'd seen a sea creature with eyes like that it had been enchanted by the Dark Queen Carlotta, and it had attacked Ella! Was it the killer whale again, come back to try to see off Molly and Delphi this time?

"Delphi!" Molly hissed, her voice coming out shaky and frightened. "Delphi, look! I think the Dark Queen's killer whale is coming for us!"

Delphi flicked her head round to see, and a look of terror crossed her face. "That's no killer whale," she said. "It's a shark, Molly. A great white shark!"

Chapter Four

Molly was terrified. She knew that the great white shark was one of the deadliest creatures in the ocean. And if those red eyes were anything to go by, it was one of the Dark Queen's servants as well, like the killer whale had been. She and Delphi were in serious trouble!

The shark was swimming towards the wreck at great speed now, and the two frightened mermaids looked at one another.

"It could out-swim us any day," Delphi said shakily. "Our only hope is your conch, Molly. Can you think of a way it could help us get rid of the shark?"

Molly was so frightened, her mind went blank at Delphi's question. But after a few moments, she remembered the cutlass. That sharp, shiny cutlass. She didn't want to hurt the shark, of course – she wouldn't hurt any ocean creature – but there might be something she could do with the cutlass to see it off...if she could only think!

She dodged to the bottom of the wreck and fumbled to open the chest again, then grabbed the jewelled cutlass handle, her fingers shaking. It felt heavy and solid in her grasp as she quickly returned to Delphi's side. Then, as the shark swam towards the mast, an idea finally came to her. She gripped her conch with her free hand and cried out, "Conch! Help me cut through wood!"

The conch glowed with a bright pink light for a moment, and so did the cutlass, its jewels sparkling and glittering through the murky water. Then, holding her breath and praying this would work, Molly swung the cutlass blade at the mast with all her might.

"Go for it, Molly!" Delphi called out.

Molly was braced for the cutlass to bounce back uselessly – she'd seen her dad sawing logs before and knew that cutting through wood was hard work. But the cutlass sliced through the old oak mast as easily as a hot knife through butter.

The top part of the mast teetered where it had been cut, and Delphi shoved it forcefully in the shark's direction. *Crash!* Down it fell, with the crossbeams toppling to the seabed, neatly trapping the shark in the rigging.

The angry shark bit at the rigging with its sharp teeth, its red eyes furious. Molly felt faint at the sight of all those rows of curving, vicious teeth inside the mighty creature's jaws, but it couldn't seem to free itself.

"Well done!" Delphi cried, throwing her arms around Molly. "Let's go back to the sea urchin, quick. We need to get my conch so I can stop that oil tanker!"

"Will the shark be all right?" Molly asked uncertainly. Even though it was a scary creature, she didn't want it to come to any harm.

"It'll be fine," Delphi assured her. "It's not hurt. Sooner or later, it'll chomp its way through the ropes. But by then, we'll be long gone. Come on!"

Delphi grabbed Molly's hand and the two mermaids swam back towards the sea urchin. "I hope we won't be too late," Molly said. "What if the Dark Queen has got to it before us?"

"Don't say that," Delphi begged. "We *must* get my shell. Look – there's the oil tanker – and it's even closer to the rocks now." Her face was pale. "If the oil is spilled, it will kill so many of our creatures – birds, fish, even dolphins and seals – by poisoning them or covering them in the sticky oil. We've got to stop it with my conch piece, Molly. We've just got to!" she said desperately, swimming faster than ever.

Delphi looked almost sick with worry, and Molly felt she had to take charge. "Come on, let's hurry on to the sea urchin, then," she said. "And if he's still being difficult, I'll just grab him off your shell. I don't care about a few spikes!" she added, trying to sound brave. Really, though, she was nervous. The sea urchin had such sharp-looking spines, it would be like picking up an aggressive hedgehog. But she'd have to do it now, however much it hurt. They had to save that oil tanker from crashing!

The two mermaids reached the craggy rock where the sea urchin had made its home and – thank goodness! – Delphi's shell was still visible beneath it. Molly took the silver dish from Delphi's bag and held it out temptingly to the spiky little creature. "Here you go," she said in her most coaxing voice. "Do you want to try this for size?"

The sea urchin hesitated for a moment, and Molly held her breath. *Please!* she willed it in her head. *Please just move!*

"Go on, it's really beautiful," she urged. "I bet your spines will look extra-bright on it." Still there was no movement from the sea urchin. Was it just being obstinate?

She was about to try one last time to persuade it when she suddenly saw its spines twitch. And then, one by one, they all began rotating, pushing the sea urchin along the rock at quite a rapid speed. Molly and Delphi exchanged hopeful glances as the sea urchin, spines rippling, propelled itself off the shell and onto the silver dish.

Delphi's hand hovered near her shell. "Well?" she asked, rather impatiently. "Is that all right?"

The sea urchin gave a contented sort of wriggle on the silver. "Very nice," it said in a pleased-sounding voice. "Very comfortable."

Molly let her breath out in a great rush of relief. "Brilliant," she said, setting the dish down on the seabed. "And your spines do look wonderful against the silver."

Delphi grinned at Molly and stretched out an arm for her conch shell. "So I'll take this now, thanks very much!"

"Oh, of course," the sea urchin said. "Do take it away. Not half as nice as my new dish."

Delphi was hardly listening, though. As she tugged at her conch piece in the rock crevice, it glowed a bright gold. Molly's shell was shining with light too, and she held it tightly, remembering that its magic had helped Ella retrieve her shell from the underwater cave.

"Oh yes!" cheered Delphi, as her shell came away smoothly in her hand, shining with an even brighter golden light. Sparks shot out from all around it, lighting up trails in the water as far as the eye could see. It almost looked like a firework in Delphi's cupped hands, Molly thought, her eyes dazzled by the sight.

"Oh, it's good to have this back," Delphi said happily. She lifted it to her cheek and pressed it against her face. "And now we must use its magic to stop the oil tanker. Come on, Molly. We need to get as close as we can!"

Molly hastened after her friend, whose silver tail was already pushing her through the sea like a glittering torpedo. "The current isn't so strong now," Molly shouted as they swam.

Delphi looked back over her shoulder with a faint smile. "The magic of my conch is working properly again, now it's back with me," she said. "It's made the current calmer, so it should be easier for us to guide the oil tanker away from the rocks. Let's just hope we can get to it in time!"

But as she spoke, there was a terrible sound of scraping metal in the distance. The mermaids peered anxiously ahead to see the bottom of the oil tanker dragging against the rocks.

"Oh no!" Delphi cried in horror. "We're too late!"

Chapter Five

"What shall we do?" cried Molly.

"We'll have to turn the direction of the current so that we can push the tanker off the rocks," Delphi said decisively, and grabbed Molly's hand. "The magic is more powerful if we join together," she said. "Hold your conch and concentrate!"

Molly did as she was told, gripping her conch with her free hand until pink sparkly magic spiralled through her fingers.

"By the power of the conch, turn the current!" Delphi cried out. Magic crackled from her shell too, but the oil tanker didn't move. "Again," she said to Molly. "Let's say it together."

Molly held her conch, willing the magic to work with all her energy. "By the power of the conch, turn the current!" the two mermaids shouted as one.

The tanker scraped against the rocks a second time. The sound of metal on stone was dreadful. Molly could hardly bear to look – she was so sure that black, sticky oil was about to come leaking from the tanker.

"The current has turned, but I just don't know if it's strong enough to move the tanker away," Delphi fretted. "It's so heavy."

"Is there anything else that could move it?" Molly wondered aloud. She remembered how she'd levered up the lid of the treasure chest with a mussel shell. "Maybe if we could find something to push it along? I'm not sure what though…"

Delphi snapped her fingers suddenly, her eyes bright. "A friendly whale!" she said. "One of the humpbacks would help us, I'm sure." She put her

forefinger and thumb into her mouth and blew a series of piercing whistles. Then she scanned the water hopefully. "If any of the humpback whales are around, they should come to my call," she said.

Molly couldn't help thinking about the scary killer whale she and Ella had encountered. She really hoped the humpback whales hadn't been recruited to the Dark Queen's army too. They certainly didn't need another red-eyed creature to attack them now!

But Delphi put a hand to her ear. "Listen!" she said. "They're coming. Can you hear them?"

Molly listened – and her fears were forgotten as she heard beautiful singing noises, mournful and melodic, sweeping up to high notes and down to low moaning sounds. "Is that really the whales?" she asked in surprise. She had no idea whales could make such music.

Delphi nodded. "Lovely, isn't it?" she said. "Look, here they come now. It's a whole pod – fantastic!"

In the distance, Molly could see a group of grey, white and black specks that grew larger as they approached. She could make out their shapes now, and their huge mottled flippers that sent them effortlessly through the water. The singing grew louder and the sound sent shivers down Molly's spine. *I will never forget this*, she thought to herself in wonder.

Moments later, the pod of whales had reached the mermaids. It was quite something to have so many large creatures massing before you, Molly thought, feeling overwhelmed at their size. They were close enough now that she could see great scars and scratches on their skin, and barnacles crusted over their bodies. They all had throat grooves running from their chins to their bellies, and deep notches in their tails.

The whales fell silent as Delphi sang back to them. Molly guessed she was explaining the problem with the tanker, because all the whales suddenly turned towards its vast dark hull as it swayed in the water. Then, when Delphi had finished her last note, the pod of whales moved as one to the tanker and pushed at it with their mighty heads.

Molly gripped her conch again, not knowing what else to do. "By the power of the conch, help the whales," she murmured under her breath. She knew they were taking a risk, coming so close to the tanker that might at any moment start leaking toxic oil.

She could hardly bear to think about what the consequences could be – they were too awful.

Her conch glittered again and a flood of sparkly light shone out, streaking through the water around the whales. Molly watched anxiously as the whales pushed...and pushed...

"It's moving!" Delphi cried. She was also holding her conch very tightly. "I'm sure it's moving!"

Molly stared. Delphi was right. Slowly, very slowly, the force of the whales combined with the current was shifting the oil tanker away from the rocks. The tanker settled in the water as the whales pushed and shoved at it, and then it began to drift away as the current caught it. A muffled cheer floated down through the water to them and Molly realized, for the first time, that there were sailors on board who must have been just as fearful as she and Delphi had been.

The whales kept on pushing the tanker along until it was a safe distance from the rocks. Then they backed off and watched it sail away.

Delphi threw her arms around Molly. "They did it!" she cried, her voice catching with relief.

"They were amazing," Molly said. "But so were you for thinking of asking them to help."

Delphi gave her a smile. "*We* did it," she said, correcting herself.

"All together. What a team!" The whales waited as the oil tanker began moving off in the opposite direction of its own accord. Then they turned, their bodies gleaming, and began jumping up through the water, their heads breaking the surface and returning with a slapping sound.

"What are they doing?" Molly asked, marvelling at the whales' acrobatics.

Delphi smiled. "It's called breaching," she replied. "They're playing." She sang out to them in the special whale language and waved. "Thank you!" she called, smiling.

The whales waved their great long flippers back at the mermaids, and swam away, some of them still making graceful breaching movements, which sent ripples of water in their wake. Molly heard their haunting singing start up again as they went.

"Good old humpbacks," Delphi said fondly. "Lovely creatures." She smiled at Molly. "Have you got enough energy to swim with me to the Undersea Kingdom?" she asked. "We must tell the Merqueen that we've found my conch, and that it's safe from the Dark Queen."

"Sure," Molly said, eager to visit the place where all the mermaids lived again. "I'd like to."

"Great," Delphi said. She slipped her conch into the pretty green bag she wore, and looked confused for a moment as she pulled something else out. It was one of the gold doubloons from the shipwreck. "Oh, I'd forgotten about these," she said. She pressed it into Molly's hand. "Here, you should have it," she said. "A souvenir from the pirate wreck!"

Molly stared in delight at the solid golden coin in her hand. Her fingers closed around it and she smiled gratefully at Delphi. "Thank you," she said.

"This has been such an exciting adventure!"

"Let's go and tell the Merqueen all about it," Delphi said. "Come on!"

Molly followed her friend through the water. It was so much easier to swim now that the storm had died down and the current wasn't so turbulent. It felt like no time before Molly could see the golden gates ahead, marking the entrance to the mermaids' kingdom.

Delphi took a small golden key from a pocket in her bag and unlocked the gates, then ushered Molly inside. She took Molly by the hand and led her through the kingdom towards the Merqueen's palace, a tall, grand building carved from white rock, with decorative towers and balconies.

Queen Luna must have been watching out for arrivals, for she swam through the mother-of-pearl palace doors to greet them almost at once, her dark blue cape billowing out behind her. Molly thought the Merqueen was one of the most beautiful beings she'd ever met, with her kindly eyes, and her chestnut hair coiled so regally on her head. The Merqueen was followed by her daughter, Princess Silva.

Delphi's face was wreathed in smiles as she greeted them. "We've got my piece of the conch!" she declared happily, taking it out of her green bag and holding it up in the air.

"Oh, my dears, that's splendid news!" Queen Luna cried, coming over and embracing first Delphi and then Molly. Over the Merqueen's shoulder, Molly could see Princess Silva's face – and was shocked to see the bitter twist of the young princess's mouth. Why wasn't Silva happy?

The princess seemed to feel Molly's eyes
upon her and started as she realized she was
being observed, quickly putting on a fake smile.
But Molly wasn't convinced. The smile didn't
reach the princess's dark eyes. Something was
wrong – but what?

Chapter Six

Delphi didn't seem to have noticed anything
unusual about the princess; she was far too busy
recounting their adventure to the Merqueen.
"And Molly was amazing! She thought of this
brilliant plan to stop the shark from attacking
us – it had been enchanted by Carlotta, I'm
sure, because it had the spookiest red eyes – and
then we called the humpbacks to help us stop an
oil tanker crashing, and…"

Molly looked towards the princess again, but she was swimming back into the palace. *Strange,* she thought to herself. *I hope she's all right.*

Queen Luna was smiling as the words tumbled breathlessly out of Delphi's mouth. "Well done, both of you," she said. "It's really wonderful to have three pieces of the conch safe from the Dark Queen. Let's hope Pearl, Coral and Shivana can bring us good news soon, too. Molly, once again, you've been a great help. Thank you, my dear."

Molly felt herself grow
warm with pride at
Queen Luna's words.
She bobbed a little
curtsy, blushing.
"You're welcome,
Your Majesty,"
she said. "I'm just
glad I could help."
"You certainly
did that." Queen
Luna smiled. "And
now it's time for you
to return to your own
world, secret mermaid.
Dawn is breaking."
"But—" Molly put in. She hated being sent
back home – especially when there were still three
other pieces of the conch left to find!

The Merquen put her hands gently on Molly's shoulders. "We will see you again soon, I promise," she said. "But for now... farewell."

"Goodbye," Molly said, a little sadly. She hugged Delphi one last time and dropped into another curtsy before the queen. Then she was surrounded by electric-blue sparkles of mermaid magic and felt as if she were being pulled very fast to the surface of the water, with the Undersea Kingdom blurring before her eyes.

The next thing she knew was the feeling of sunlight on her face through a gap in the curtains. She rubbed her eyes and sat up to see a shaft of white morning light on her bedroom floor. The sight was enough to make her scramble out of bed at once – a sunny day, after all the storms they'd had recently! – but as she moved, she realized she was holding something.

She uncurled her fingers to see a gold coin in her palm…and the adventures of the night before came rushing back into her mind. A pirate doubloon from the shipwreck! Oh, it had been so exciting! Way better than any dream she could have had.

She went to the window and stared out at the sea. It looked flat and smooth now, sparkling a glorious blue in the early morning sunlight.

Perfect weather for going down to the beach, she thought to herself with a happy stretch.

Molly couldn't stop smiling as she put on her dressing gown, and all but skipped down to the breakfast table.

"Hello, Molly," her mum said, pouring her a drink of orange juice. "Have you seen what Toby's got this morning?"

Molly turned to look at her baby brother, who was sitting in his high chair, banging a plastic spoon on the tray and grinning. There, on his lower gum, was a single white tooth, just peeking out from the pink. "Oh, Toby!" she exclaimed. "Your first tooth!" She bent down to look at it and he beamed obligingly, as if showing it off.

Molly couldn't help thinking about the shark's teeth she'd seen with Delphi. She was glad her baby brother's teeth weren't quite so sharp!

"Isn't it a lovely morning?" Molly's gran said just then, coming into the room slowly, leaning on her stick. "I can't believe it, when it was so stormy last night. The clouds have melted away as if by magic."

Molly grinned at her gran while her mum's back was turned. "As if by magic," she echoed, and winked.

Then she settled down to her breakfast with a smile on her face. A day on the beach today, and another mermaid adventure to look forward to soon... She truly felt like the luckiest girl in the world.

The End

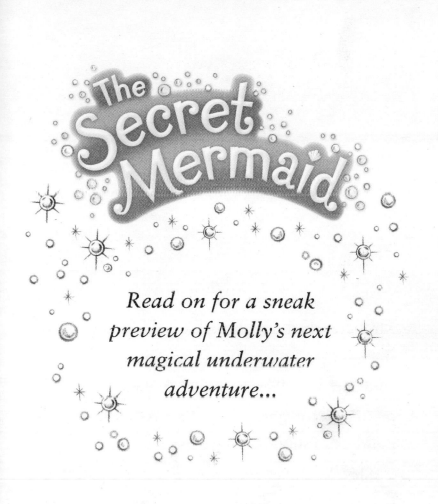

The Secret Mermaid

Read on for a sneak
preview of Molly's next
magical underwater
adventure...

Reef Rescue

Molly reached out and took hold of her conch shell, wrapping her fingers around its smooth, cool surface. "Please, please take me to the mermaids tonight," she whispered, holding it tightly. "I think they need me."

She closed her eyes and lay listening to the sea. *Sssshhhh... Ssssshhhhh... Sssshhhh...* went the waves as they rolled in and out.

And then, without any warning, Molly felt as

if she were falling very fast from a great height. She could hear a rushing sound in her ears as she fell further and further, faster and faster...

"Molly... Molly... Molly..." called a voice, very faint, as if someone was shouting to her from far away.

Molly felt tingles all over as the falling sensation stopped, and she opened her eyes at last. She was on the seabed, with warm, azure water around her. Molly gasped in excitement and immediately gazed down at herself. Yes! She was wearing a turquoise top with her conch necklace around her throat, and where her legs had been, there now swung a sparkling green-scaled tail. She was a secret mermaid again – the shell's magic had worked!

"Molly... Molly..." The voice came again – louder this time. Molly swung around to see one of the Shell-Keeper mermaids swimming towards her. It was Coral, smiling and waving, her dark hair streaming behind her and her violet eyes bright and welcoming. "Molly!" she cried, greeting her with a hug. "Oh, I'm so pleased to see you."

Molly hugged her back. "I'm glad to be here," she said – and then saw over Coral's shoulder where she was. "Oh," she said. "We're in the coral reef!"

Coral nodded, and the smile vanished from her face. "Yes," she said, "and doesn't it look awful?" She flung an arm out, pointing around them. "Look – parts of the reef have become bleached, do you see? All the algae have gone, and without them the reef doesn't have enough energy to feed all the creatures that come here."

Molly gazed around. The coral structures of the reef were skeletal and white, and looked rather eerie, looming through the sea like ghostly fingers in every direction. The whole place seemed deserted.

"It wasn't so long ago that this reef was seething with life," Coral went on miserably. "There were all kinds of colourful fish – clownfish, rays and pufferfish – plus there were sand sharks, sea cows, eels, squid, sea turtles…" Her voice trailed away. "And now they've all left to find new homes – if they can. Oh, if only I had my piece of the conch! I could work some healing magic to bring this reef back to life. But I still haven't found it – and I've been looking for days now!"

"I'll help you look," Molly said, wanting to comfort her.

Coral gave a weak smile. "Thank you," she said. "I heard from the other Shell-Keepers that you've been amazing at helping them."

Molly blushed with pride. She knew that

Carlotta, the bad mermaid queen, had originally stolen the five magical conch pieces from the Shell-Keeper mermaids, and taken them back to her dark cave. But when Molly first entered the Undersea Kingdom, the magic of Molly's sixth piece of the conch had sent the shell pieces scattering through the ocean. With Molly's help, Ella and Delphi had already found their pieces of the magical conch. Molly really hoped she could help Coral find hers too, in time to save the reef from dying out completely.

She felt a swishing sensation behind her just then and turned to see an enormous sea turtle gliding serenely through the water towards the two mermaids. "Oh!" Molly cried, delighted at the sight of such a huge, graceful creature. "Hello there."

The sea turtle had dark beady eyes and a wide, friendly smile, but she looked

concerned. She sailed right up to Molly and
Coral, her flipper-like legs moving strongly
through the water. Her green shell was large
and heart-shaped, with yellowy edging.

"Hello," she said in a low, musical voice.
"Have you seen my baby? I can't find him
anywhere – the reef seems deserted."

Coral shook her head. "No, I haven't seen
any creatures in this part of the reef for a
while," she said, with rather a sad sigh. "I don't
know where they've all gone."

The sea turtle gave a slow blink. "The sea
horses say that there's one area of the reef that's
still healthy – Tropical Valley, they're calling
it," she replied. "And you know what the sea
horses are like – they seem to hear everything
first! So that's where I'm headed, just as soon
as I can find my little one. He's still very small,
and doesn't have a good sense of direction. I'm

worried he's got lost, or stuck somewhere."

Molly bent to stroke the old turtle's head. "We'll look out for him," she promised. "I'm sure he can't have gone too far."

"Thank you," the turtle said. She waved goodbye with her flipper, and swam slowly away.

Molly and Coral watched her disappear into the damaged reef. "Maybe we should head for Tropical Valley too," Coral suggested thoughtfully. "If the reef is healthy there, it may mean my shell is somewhere close by." She shrugged. "You never know, some of the magic might have leaked out and be helping to protect that part of the reef."

Molly nodded. "We should definitely take a look," she said. "And if all the other creatures have taken refuge there, you could ask if any of them have seen your shell."

She and Coral swam away from the silent, empty reef, and Molly felt a shiver of relief as they left it behind. There was something very sad about being there – it felt as if they'd been standing in the ruins of an old house, hollow and lifeless, with nothing but ghosts and memories around them.

She gave herself a little shake. There was no point getting miserable and downcast about it – she and Coral had work to do. If they could find Coral's piece of conch shell, they would be able to help the reef flourish once more, and…

Molly was jerked out of her thoughts by a sudden scream. She glanced around to see Coral being dragged away from her by a strong whirling current. "Come back!" she yelled, without thinking, striking out after her friend. But seconds later, she regretted it. For now, she was being pulled along by the mighty torrent of water too – and however hard Molly battled against it, she was powerless to swim in any other direction.

It felt as if she were fighting the water, scrabbling at it with her arms, thrashing at it with her tail…but to no end. Nothing she did made any difference – she was trapped in the rushing current with Coral as it threw them roughly along. Was this something to do with the Dark Queen?

To find out what happens next, read

To find out more
about Molly and all her
mermaid friends, and have
some magical ocean fun,
check out

www.thesecretmermaid.co.uk

The Secret Mermaid

Far out in the ocean live the Shell-Keeper mermaids. While the rest of the world sleeps, one little girl joins them for some magical mermaid adventures.

Collect all of Molly's magical mermaid quests

Enchanted Shell 9780746096154

Molly is transported to the Undersea Kingdom for the first time, where she discovers she is the secret mermaid!

Seaside Adventure 9780746096161

To help Ella recover her piece of the magical conch, Molly must find a way to trap an angry killer whale.

Underwater Magic 9780746096178

Can Molly find some pirate treasure to win back
Delphi's shell from a grumpy sea urchin?

Reef Rescue 9780746096192

Molly must help Coral find her shell to restore
the ocean reefs, but a swarm of jellyfish stands
in their way...

Deep Trouble 9780746096185

Pearl's conch piece is trapped in an undersea volcano
and guarded by sea snakes. How can she and
Molly release it?

Return of the Dark Queen 9780746096208

Molly must save Shivana from an Arctic prison before
the Shell-Keeper mermaids can finally face the Dark
Queen and complete the magical conch.

Oliver Moon
Junior Wizard

Collect all of Oliver Moon's magical adventures!

Oliver Moon and the Potion Commotion

Can Oliver create a potion to win the Young Wizard of the Year award?

ISBN 9780746073063

Oliver Moon and the Dragon Disaster

Oliver's sure his new pet dragon will liven up the Festival of Magic...

ISBN 9780746073070

Oliver Moon and the Nipperbat Nightmare

Things go horribly wrong when Oliver gets to look after the school pet.

ISBN 9780746077917

Oliver Moon's Summer Howliday

Oliver suspects there is something odd about his hairy new friend, Wilf.

ISBN 9780746077924

Oliver Moon's Christmas Cracker

Can a special present save Oliver's Christmas at horrible Aunt Wart's?

ISBN 9780746077931

Oliver Moon and the Spell-off

Oliver must win a spell-off against clever Casper to avoid a scary forfeit.

ISBN 9780746077948

Oliver Moon's Fangtastic Sleepover

Will Oliver survive a school sleepover in the haunted house museum?

ISBN 9780746084793

Oliver Moon and the Broomstick Battle

Can Oliver beat Bully to win the Junior Wizards' Obstacle Race?

ISBN 9780746084809

Happy Birthday, Oliver Moon

Will Oliver's birthday party be ruined when his invitations go astray?

ISBN 9780746086872

Oliver Moon and the Spider Spell

Oliver's Grow-bigger spell lands the Witch Baby's pet in huge trouble.

ISBN 9780746090749

Oliver Moon and the Troll Trouble

Can Oliver save the show as the scary, stinky troll in the school play?

ISBN 9780746086865

Oliver Moon and the Monster Mystery

Strange things start to happen when Oliver wins a monster raffle prize...

ISBN 9780746090756

Sue Mongredien has published over 60 books, including the magical *Oliver Moon, Junior Wizard* series. Like Molly Holmes, Sue loves exploring, and gave up a job as an editor of children's books to travel the world, before becoming a full-time writer. Sue also loves the sea, and had a house near Brighton beach before moving to Bath, where she now lives with her husband and three children.